Unbroken
(Shattered Promis-
es, #2.5)

JESSICA SORENSEN

For information:

Jessicasorensen.com

Cover Design: Mae I Design

http://www.maeidesign.com/

Unbroken—2.5

ISBN: 978-1494306588

Chapter 1

(Alex)

I'm trying not to fucking freak out, but Gemma's been gone for hours. It's driving me literally crazy and that dying feeling that I get whenever we're apart for too long is starting to surface. The electricity dwindles. Tiredness sets in.

I miss her. Need her here—want her here. I've never wanted anything this badly before and it's confusing the shit out of me.

"Alex, would you please try to relax?" my sister, Aislin, begs while she watches me pace the small living room, raking my fingers through my brown hair over and over again as I veer toward the brink of insanity.

"I can't," I tell her, quickening my pacing despite how tired I'm getting; the energy draining from my body. "You don't get it. I can't even think straight."

She shifts on the sofa, leaning forward to grab a bottle of water from the coffee table.

We're at the beach house where we've been sitting for hours, waiting for Gemma or Laylen to show up, but they're both missing. Part of me is worried they're together; that when Gemma went looking for Laylen, she found him, and then they wandered off to do God knows what. I actually have a few ideas. Ideas that make my blood burn beneath my skin. My muscles tighten. My fists clench. The need to smash them into something is so overwhelming that it takes a lot of control not to go over to the wall and punch it.

Then there's always the other alternative, and that one makes me ache. That something did happened to her. That maybe the Death Walkers got a hold of her. Or Demetrius. Or maybe my father. It's the one explanation I don't want to admit. I hate thinking of him as evil, but not because I don't believe he is. I do. It's more because it's been en-grained in my mind to think of him as being good.

Everything he's said I've had to agree was right oth-erwise I'd be punished, and even though I'm a Keeper and have a higher pain tolerance than the average person, my father is an Immortal and is way stronger than I am. The punches. The kicks. Being whipped. Locked up without food. The torture. It wasn't easy to endure. If I cried, he'd only make my life more of a living hell, so I learned not to cry. Not to feel pain. Not to feel anything. Yes, sir. That's how I learned to be around him.

Now, though… everything's all screwed up. I think even when I was younger, deep down I knew there was something messed up about my father, more than just the beatings. But I didn't think he'd been working against eve-rything the Keepers represent, which is to protect humanity, not destroy it.

"Oh, for the love of God. I can't watch this anymore." Aislin gets up from the sofa and steps in front of my pac-ing path and I have slam to a stop, almost running over her, and she has to step back. "Would you settle down? You're seriously going to wear a hole in the floor."

"That's the stupidest fucking thing I've ever heard." My tone is clipped, but that's just how Aislin and I are together. We're brother and sister. We fight. We're rude to each other. Deep down, however, I'd never want anything to happen to her. In fact, a lot of the times when she'd get in trouble as a child, I'd take the fall and the beatings to spare her the pain. I can handle it better anyway. "And I can't settle down." I swing around her and continue pacing the length of the room. "If I do, then I'll lose my mind."

She sighs and then sinks down on the armrest of the sofa. "I've never seen you act like this over anyone before. It's... interesting." She tucks a strand of her hair behind her ear. "And really unsettling."

"I know." I fold my arms across my chest as I continue pacing, pacing, pacing. "I'm not even sure what's causing it... I just feel so..." I trail off. I fucking hate talking about my feelings. After an emotionally numb childhood, I find it easier not to feel anything at all, but with Gemma...

Well, it's out of my hands. Although I'm not one hundred percent sure what exactly I feel for her yet, it's really confusing and intense amongst a thousand other things.

"So what?" Aislin wonders curiously. "Because I'm dying to know."

I raise my eyebrows questioningly at her. "Why?"

"Because in the twenty-five years that I've known you, I've never seen you act like this over someone." She sits back down and crosses her legs. "And I find it fascinating."

I open my mouth to try to explain it to her, but then realize I don't want to and probably couldn't even if I tried. My thoughts jumble as I attempt to sort through everything going on in my head. "Why the hell are you so calm?" I change the subject. "Laylen's missing, too."

She swallows nervously, like she's just realizing this. "I know."

"We need to do something." I stop in front of the window and glance outside at the front yard. It's dark, though the stars and moon are bright in the sky. I remember all the times when I was a child and Gemma and I would look at the stars, obsessed with them. It makes sense now that I know we're both carrying around the energy of a fallen star, but at the time I just thought we were two weird kids that understood each other. "We need a plan to figure out where she is."

"I could do a locating spell," Aislin suggests as I turn away from the window. "But I'd have to run to a Wicca Shop because my supplies are really low."

"Yeah, that might work," I mutter, trying to get myself to focus on fixing the problem instead of just the situation itself.

"*Might* work," Aislin says arrogantly, getting to her feet. "You mean it *will* work."

I'm not so confident, considering the many spells I've witnessed go awry over the years. Still, I collect the car keys from the coffee table. "You drive to the Wicca Shop." I toss her the keys and she catches them. "I'll stay here just in case one of them comes back."

She throws the car keys back at me, scowling. "Or I could just transport like a normal witch. Jesus, you are really out of it, aren't you? You need to get your head into the game or we aren't going to get anywhere."

"Yeah, maybe," I mutter, tucking the car keys into my pocket. She's right. I need to focus. "Alright, I think I'll go search the beach some more while you go get supplies." I cross the living room, heading for the back door that's in the kitchen. "Meet you back here in a bit?" I ask and she nods, walking toward the hallway that leads to her bedroom.

After I grab a flashlight, I walk out of the house and step off the porch onto the sandy beach. I start to relax a little. Fresh air. The sound of the waves crashing against the shore. It's distracting and relaxes me slightly from my worries. If only I could make the goddamn stars go away, then maybe I could completely clear my head.

Hiking down the shoreline dotted with beach houses while sweeping the flashlight from side to side, I look for any sign of Gemma or Laylen. There are no fresh foot-

prints nearby—nothing at all—and this ridiculous, helpless feeling emerges inside me. It's not the first time I've
felt it. In fact, I've felt it a few times.

Once when I was younger and my father was getting
ready to detach Gemma's soul, something he hadn't told
me until later on in life when I was more brainwashed and
would react less. I had felt helpless watching her leave,
knowing I'd never see her again and I was too young to do
anything. I also felt the same way when I was reunited
with her at the college campus. The first time she touched
me again and I didn't think I could have her, yet I wanted
her so fucking bad. The last time had been at the cabin in
Colorado while I was waiting for my father to show up
and detach her soul again. I didn't want to let it happen,
yet I was torn between what I had thought was right and
wrong. I ended up doing what I thought at the time was
the wrong thing and tried to flee with her. Then my father
showed up with the Death Walkers and I realized that everything I'd thought was wrong might just be right.

My head is swimming with the helpless sensation by
the time I arrive at the end of the beach where a cluster of

rocks blocks me from getting any further. I'm about to head back when I hear the soft sound of footsteps move up from behind me. I turn around and startle back when my flashlight highlights a very familiar face.

"Gemma?" I pause, shining the light into her strikingly beautiful eyes, feeling a wave of electricity rush over me from the connection we share. But whether it's from the star or something else, though, I'm unsure.

I immediately sense there's something off about her. It definitely looks like Gemma, but there's something missing…. Something's vanished from the last time I've seen her. She looks so hollow, and the sparks are merely a lull of warmth; nowhere near as intense as they usually are. It's how I've imagined she looked when her soul was detached, and the thought of it sends a chill up my spine.

I reach out to grab her, but she quickly raises her arm, moving way faster than she normally does; the sparks suddenly going haywire. Before I can tell what's happening, there's a shovel in her hand, and seconds later, something smacks me in the head. Hard. With way more strength then Gemma has ever possessed before. The flashlight slips from my hands and I raise my arm as I stagger, the number of stars in the sky multiplying. She easily dodges my advances and swings the shovel back around, hitting me on the head again. I've taken a lot of beatings and know that I won't go down without at least a few more hits, but I need to get my shit together.

I work to get my footing and blink my vision back into focus, then hurry away from her. I just need a few seconds to get the dizziness and the throbbing ache out of my head, and then I can concentrate. But she easily chases after me, her long legs moving quicker than I remember as she runs through the sand.

Shit.

I dodge to the side and then try to circle around her, but she matches my moves and we end up colliding. She drops the shovel as our legs tangle together as we both lose our balance and fall toward the sand. I instinctively grab onto her, wanting to protect her from the fall despite the fact that she has just hit me in the head with a shovel.

She lands on top of me with a leg on each side, her breasts pressing against my chest, her lips inches from mine, and my fingers digging into her waist to support her weight. There's a brief pause where I feel so turned on; not just by the feel of her, but from the pain, which is extremely fucked up. It's not the first time it's happened, either.

"What the hell is wrong with you?" I ask as she pushes back and sits up on top of me.

She doesn't say a word. She just lifts her arm above her, the glow of the moon hitting her hauntingly empty expression. That's when I spot it; the triangular mark on her forearm. It feels like every part of me has died. My heart stops beating. My lungs stop working.

"No," I whisper.

She simply smiles in response and I know what I have to do. I hate it, though I have no choice. It's either do this or kill her. So I channel all my inner strength and flip us over so she's lying on her back in the sand. She struggles, kicking and trying to knee me in the gut, but I restrain her by the shoulders, pinning her down.

15

"Relax, I'm not going to hurt you," I say as she writhes her body beneath me. "I'm just going to make this a little easier on me."

She pauses and then starts to laugh, her chest heaving, hot and feisty sparks seem to flow from her, and my skin feels like it's on fire. "Oh, my God. You think you can hurt me." Her laughter cuts off so quickly that it's creepy. "Don't be ridiculous." Then she dips her head to the side and her teeth graze my skin.

I hate what I'm about to do—hate that I'm controlling her in any way, shape or form—but I still clear my head and prepare myself to take her energy away, making her exhausted. She doesn't know that I can do this to people—make them disoriented—only because I'm afraid of what she'll do if she finds out. She's big on trust, which is un-derstandable, and this is downright manipulation. I don't do it very often, but it's the only thing I can think of to do at the moment.

Taking a deep breath, I gradually start draining her strength, forcing her to become weak and drowsy, careful to only drain enough that she gets sluggish yet doesn't pass out. Her eyes start to roll into her head, but then she manages to get one of her hands up and grabs ahold of my arm. She starts clawing at my skin, splitting it open over and over again. Blood pours out and trickles down my forearm. She starts laughing at the sight of it. It's an annoying laugh that doesn't belong to her and sounds more like it belongs to a hyena. Her head is tipped back in the sand, her hair surrounding her head, while she totally disregards me as if I couldn't conquer her.

"You stupid, little boy," she says, shaking my head. "You never can do anything right."

And just like that, something snaps inside me. Breaks. Shatters. I see red as she utters the words my father used to say to me all the time.

"Fuck it," I growl, and then quickly and callously drain all the energy out of her. Her eyes widen for a split second, however she has no time to react, and seconds later she blacks out.

She's still breathing. Still alive. But she also still has the Mark of Evil branded on her.

Chapter 2

(Alex)

After Gemma goes unconscious, lying dazedly in the sand below me, I hop off her and scoop her up, carrying her toward the house. Her arm with the Mark of Evil hangs lifelessly to the side and her head bobbles around with my movements. I feel vaguely bad for what I've done to her, but at the same time, there was no other choice. Do what you have to, no matter the cost. That's what I was taught to do, and although sometimes I hate it, it's times like these where I'm glad I don't think twice.

When I get inside the house, I gently put her on the sofa in the living room. Aislin's still gone, so I sit and wait for her while thinking of any possible way to fix this along with how the hell it has happened to begin with. The Mark of Malefiscus is only supposed to appear on those that are of evil descent, and Gemma can't be; there's no way.

So how did it get there? Did it appear like a normal mark does? Or did Nicholas have something to do with this? That damn Faerie seems to have some sick obsession with her. Or maybe it's my father who put it on her. Is that where she disappeared to for the last few hours? Has he had her trapped while she's been missing?

As she lies there, out of it on the sofa, I stroke her cheek softly. We used to be so close, but now it seems like we barely know each other anymore. It's my own damn fault for letting everything get between us. A childhood friendship, one made of promises to be friends forever. Then, just because my father had said so, I'd let it go. And now I want it back. I want to tell her what we had... What I want... What do I want?

As I'm trying to figure that out, she starts to stir. I hold onto her arms, figuring I'll let her come out of her daze before I put her back under so she can have a few minutes to recuperate. Suddenly, though, like the snap of a lightning bolt, her eyes shoot open and she springs upward onto the sofa. Our foreheads slam together like bricks smashing together. I fall off the edge of the sofa, blinking my eyes as my head starts to buzz, however Gemma doesn't miss a beat. She jumps up and lands on top of me, crouched over me like a cave woman.

"I have to kill you," she says in a numb voice, her hair hanging over her face, a rabid look in her eyes.

My fingers wrap around her wrists. "No, you don't." I know it's probably useless to reason with her, but I have to try. "Just back off me and as soon as Aislin gets here, we'll get you taken care of." I hope.

She laughs that snide laugh I'm not fond of while throwing her head back. "Take care of me. Don't be absurd." She lowers her head, cocking it to the side as she eyes me over. "Besides, I don't know why you'd want to change me." She lowers her hips so she's straddling me, then she places a hand on each side of my head. "I figured you'd like me like this better." She leans in, her violet eyes looking more like a shade of dark lavender veering toward black. "Think of the things I could do to you." She grabs my shoulders and her nails pierce my skin through the fabric of my shirt, drawing blood, and for a split moment, sheer ecstasy flows through my body… Maybe she knows me better than I thought, knows how to get under my skin… maybe I should let her…

I shake the thoughts from my head. This isn't Gemma. Just a warped, evil version of her. "Is that what you want?" I slip my hands out from her hold and grab onto her hips, pressing my fingers into her skin. "To show me the things you could do to me? Because I thought you said you had to kill me."

She seems both amused and confused by my statement, which gives me hope that my Gemma is still in there somewhere. "I don't know…" She leans closer, like she's going to kiss me. "…what I want to do." Her lips touch mine and I don't move, even when she sucks my bottom lip into her mouth and bites on it.

Fuck. This isn't her. This isn't her. That's what I keep telling myself over and over again.

But I'm about to give in, flip her over, and tear off her clothes—the feel of the sparks, pain, and scent of her too overwhelming—when her fingers wander up my chest to my throat. Grasping tightly, she starts to strangle me, her grip tight as it restricts my airway.

"Like I said," she whispers in my ear, her teeth grazing my lobe. "I have to kill you. I was just trying to have a little fun before I did." As she continues to choke me, her free hand slides down my chest to my stomach, her fingers wandering all over my body. She smiles, enjoying herself, as I reach up and grab her arm.

"I'm sorry," I whisper and her smug expression briefly falters.

"For what?" she asks, confounded.

"For this." With one swift breath, I begin to drain the energy from her body, not taking it easy on her this time. I take as much as I can until her eyes roll into the back of her head, until her body slumps to the side, until her fingers leave my neck. Before she can fall to the floor, I hurry and sit up, catching her in my arms.

"I'm sorry," I say again because I feel bad. She's going to be out for quite a while, and when she does wake up, it's not going to be the most pleasant experience.

Gathering her in my arms, I pick her up, carry her into the bedroom, and lay her down on her bed. Then I get the ties that hold the curtains up and bind them around her wrists and ankles, securing them to the bedposts as I attempt to ignore the fact that I'm enjoying this way too much.

After staring at her for longer than I should, I head through the house to check and see if Aislin has transported back, hoping she knows a spell that can remove marks somehow. But, when I step into her room, I realize I have much bigger problems then a possessed Gemma because my ex-girlfriend is sitting on the bed.

My ex-girlfriend that has the touch of death.

Chapter 3

(Alex)

"What the fuck are you doing here?" I ask as I stop in the doorway, knowing that space is always best whenever Stasha is around.

She's sitting on the bed, her legs crossed, her blonde hair curled, and her hands covered with tan leather gloves. "Now is that any way to talk to an old lover?" she asks, faking a frown as she rises to her feet, her heels clicking against the hardwood floor.

"Old lover?" I question, bracing my hands on the doorframe. "I think you've gotten your words a little mixed up. We were never lovers, Stasha. You were just there to pass time when I was bored and I'm pretty sure you knew that."

Her fake frown deepens as she slowly strolls around Aislin's room covered with bags of herbs, candles, vials of powder and other Wicca ingredients. She's pretending to simply glance around at everything, but I know Stasha well enough to know that everything she does is calculated and she has to be looking for something.

"You know, I'd say I was hurt by what you just said." She runs her finger along the desk, pausing to look at Aislin's open spell book. "But you know me well enough to know I don't get hurt." She cocks her head to the side, reading something on one of the pages. It makes me nervous. Stasha's not a Witch, so I know she can't actually cast a spell, yet I do know her well enough to know it's not good for her to be interested in magic. Besides, if she does get a witch to cast a spell for her—which she easily could—it will be for her own benefit. And Stasha never wants anything good. Everything she does is based solely on greed.

I cross my arms and lean against the doorway. "Why are you here?"

She wavers, and then turns around with an innocent look on her face. "Who says I'm not just here to see you?"

"Why are you here?" I repeat, giving her a blank expression.

She rolls her eyes as she lets out a sigh, slumping back against the desk. "Oh, fine. Pretend to be annoyed that I'm here, but deep down I know you miss me," she replies and I can't help it, I laugh at her. She scowls at me, losing her cool.

If I'm not careful, then she could very easily take off the gloves and drain my life simply by touching me. At the same time, though, I don't want to give her the satisfaction of letting her think she has the upper hand.

"I'm sorry," I retort without any real sincerity. "Did I hurt your feelings?"

She narrows her eyes at me and seconds later she's slipping off her gloves, taking out one finger at a time, attempting to torment me. "Need I remind you what I am,

Alex?" She takes a few steps forward, holding the gloves in one hand. "What I can do?"

Despite how much I want to stand here and push her as much as I can, I also want to get her the hell out of the house. The last thing I need is a crazy ex-girlfriend of mine running around while my current girlfriend is possessed by what seems like the devil. It seems like that could be a disaster in the making.

"Tell me what you want," I say, irritated.

She gives me a conniving grin, stopping just a few steps away from me. "Not without a price. You know that."

"And why would I give you anything?" I ask, standing up straight. "Especially when I don't even know if you're here for a good reason or not."

She stretches her hands out in front of her, pretending to examine her nails. Blackish vines appear beneath her skin, curving all the way up her forearm. She's channeling her energy to make it appear as if she's about to kill me, but I still have some time before we get to that point... I think.

"Tell me something," she asks, wiggling her fingers and making the vines spread up to her shoulders, her power amplifying. "Have you by chance lost something over the last few hours?"

My muscles tighten. Shit. Does she know about Gemma? Does she have something to do with what's happened to her?

"What did you do?" I step forward, reducing the space between us as anger begins to burn under my skin. At the moment, I don't care if she canreach forward and kill me. I'm too fucking pissed at the idea that she'd be vindictive enough to do something to Gemma, though I'm really not at all surprised.

"Hey, I didn't do anything," she says, trying to be offended. "He came to me, okay?"

"*He*?" I'm confused. "Who the hell are you talking about?"

She gapes at me. "Um, the super tall, sexy vampire that I'm pretty sure belongs to you... or, well, belongs to Aislin." She pauses, a malicious look rising on her face. "Or maybe it's that star girl you've always secretly been in love with. Gamma or whatever. He did talk about her a lot." She scrunches her nose at the thought. "It would be pretty funny. The girl that you could never let go, falling in love with your best friend. Or ex-best friend anyway."

I'm not even sure what comes over me. I'm usually good with insults—especially Stasha's—yet something about Gemma and Laylen and her accusations makes me lose control of my anger. Something snaps inside me, and before I can shut it down, I'm charging toward her outstretched hands of death.

"I'd watch it if I were you," she warns, waggling her fingers, the movement just enough to cause me to freeze just inches away from them.

Composing myself, I back away from her, telling myself to settle down because I'm not going to get anywhere with any of this if I'm dead. "Either you can put the gloves back on or leave," I tell her calmly.

She rolls her eyes, but starts to put her gloves back on. "What's gotten into you?" She gets her fingers snuggly into one glove and then moves to the other hand. "You used to be so much stronger and had it together more than this while we were dating. " Once she gets the gloves on, she lowers her arms to her sides. "But you're acting so erratic."

I hate to admit it, but she's right; although I'm not going to tell her that. Just like I've never admitted anything to her during the four years I dated her.

Our relationship was built solely on one thing—sex. I got bored and went to her to fill up my time, and she was a cold enough person that she didn't mind.

In fact, sometimes I think she's as dead inside as me, but that might be because she actually has death in her.

"We haven't dated in a couple of years," I say blankly. "Things change."

She eyes me over with disgust. "And not for the bet-ter. Jesus, look at you." She crosses her arms, her face pinched. "All worked up over some girl."

"How do you know about Gemma?" I wonder. "Is it just from Laylen or has word been traveling?"

Her mouth turns up to a grin as she struts up to me. "Wouldn't you like to know?" She places a finger on my chest and traces a line all the way up to my chin. "You know, I could easily tell you if you gave me something in return." She bites her lip as her finger slides under my chin.

I lean out of her touch. "Get out," I say coldly. "I don't have time for your shit, and trust me, whatever you want from me, you're not going to get."

She scowls. "Fuck you. You don't have to be such a douche."

"I thought you liked the douche," I challenge, arching my brow.

Her face reddens with anger and I wait for her to un-leash her wrath, maybe even pull off the gloves, but instead she simmers down and steps back. "Fine. Be that way." She walks toward the back of the room and something occurs to me.

"Wait, how did you get back here?" I ask, inching into the room toward her.

She flips her hair off her shoulders as she squares them. "Oh, Alex, you really have gone downhill, haven't you? Forgetting that anything's possible." Then with a smile, she picks up Aislin's spell book. "Besides, I never even came here for you." She raises the book. "Only this."

"Shit." I run toward her, but I hit an invisible force field in the center of the room that flings me back through the air. I land on my back, the impact so intense it knocks the wind out of me. After I recover, I jump to my feet, but by the time I get up, she's gone, and I have no clue where she went or how she even got here in the first place.

This is bad. Very bad. At least from my point of view. The only way to find out for sure is for Aislin to get here and tell me what Stasha could possibly want with her spell book. I mean, she's only a Keeper with the gift of death, which she inherited from her mother who had a slight bit of Plant Nymph blood inside her.

My first instinct is to go check on Gemma, so I hurry across the house and am both relieved and frustrated when I enter the room because she's there, but she's awake.

"Don't look so disappointed to see me," she says, wiggling her arms which are still tied to the bedposts. She's trying to sit up; her head lifted so she can look at me, her hair's tangled around her face and her shirt's riding up so that her bare stomach is revealed. So sexy except for that stupid smirk on her face. "I'm not that bad to be around, am I?"

"It depends," I reply, entering the room on guard. The arrival of Stasha has reminded me that at any moment anything could happen. Besides, if Gemma's here like this, then whoever possessed her in the first place might show up here, too. "Who am I talking to?"

She laughs, rolling her eyes. "You're talking to me. Gemma Lucas. The girl I've always been. The girl that both annoys you and enthralls you. The girl you love to fuck."

"Yeah, the Gemma I know wouldn't say that," I say, walking up to the bed. "And if she did say it, her cheeks would turn pink with her embarrassment." I sit down on the bed beside her and lightly stroke her cheek with my finger. "This isn't the Gemma I know."

Her amusement rapidly shifts to anger. Turning her head, she tries to bite my finger and manages to knick the skin. "That Gemma was weak," she snaps. "This one is so much better." She shuts her eyes and breathes in deeply, like she's ravishing the taste of the air. "God, I feel so alive at the moment... like I could do anything."

It kills me to see her like this, my chest aching in a way I didn't think was possible. "Look, I don't know who you are, but you need to bring her back."

Her eyes shoot open and I'm startled by the amount of anger blazing in them, smoldering lavender. She looks as enraged as my father would get whenever Aislin or I would do something wrong. "I already told you who I am. Gemma Lucas. Nothing more. Nothing less."

"Who did this to you, then?" I ask, reaching out to touch her, yet when she scowls at me, I draw my hand away. "Who put that mark on your arm?"

She tips her chin down to look at the mark branded on her skin. "Does it really matter?" she asks. "You and I both know that regardless of how it got on there, it's on there, which means I have evil in my blood."

"No, there has to be a different reason," I insist. "Like maybe the star allowed it on you."

She shakes her head, laughing. "Don't be stupid. It's on me because I have evil blood inside me. Because I've been evil all along and this," she jerks her marked arm upward, "just allowed me to let it out."

I ball my hands into fists, fighting the urge to yell, but she's pissing me off. "I've known you since we were kids and trust me, there's not a single damn drop of evil inside you, whether you think so or not."

"That's not what your father told me," she says, watching my reaction with hunger as the desire to break me lurks within her eyes.

My fists clench tighter while my jaw goes taut; my anger begins simmering, ready to boil over the surface. "Is that who did this to you?" I ask, and although she doesn't respond, I can see it in her eyes.

I've been angry before, but this… I'm not sure I can handle the heat of emotions flaring inside me. I want to punch my father. Throttle him. Maybe even kill him. I want to hurt him so badly at the moment that it's tearing me up inside.

Getting to my feet, I storm over to the wall and hammer my fist repeatedly through it, trying to let out the anger the safest way I can think of. While the wall doesn't make it out so great, a large hole in it, no one gets hurt and the pressure inside me is alleviated just a bit.

"Feeling better?" Gemma asks as I make my way back to the bed, stretching out my fingers.

Shaking my head, I climb on the bed and align my body over her. I don't know why. It's not like I usually get this close to my enemies; yet, she's not my enemy. She's my... soul mate? Other half? I have no clue. All I know is that I need to be close to her. "Tell me what my father wants," I demand, leaning over her, trying to picture her as someone else to make this easier.

She elevates her head, getting as close to me as she can. "He wants you dead, which I will do," she hisses. "So just untie me and lets get this over with.

"You really think you can do that?" I ask, leaning closer as my fingers find her wrists. "You really think you can hurt me?"

She nods her head up and down, an arrogant look in her eyes, and I fucking hate how much I love it; love that she just might be able to hurt me. "It'd be the easiest thing I've ever done," she says haughtily.

I assess her closely, debating how much I should push her. How far should I go with this just to see how deeply she's possessed? I know the mark on her arm is powerful and it might be stupid to test it's strength against Gemma's feelings for me, but it might be the only way to get her back.

I just hope this plan doesn't backfire and I wind up dead.

Chapter 4

(Alex)

This world has always been confusing to me; life has always been confusing. It's always full of surprises and full of risks. There never seems to be a right or wrong way to solve problems, and a lot of the time problems aren't solved intentionally but by accident. I know nothing about Gemma's condition—how my father got the mark on her— so I have no idea how to get it off of her. The only thing I can do is try and hope that whatever I do works. It fucking sucks. But I have to try.

I lock eyes with her and force her to look at me. Stare at her until she becomes completely uncomfortable, which is right where I want her—confused. "So you really think you can hurt me?" I ask, stretching my arm toward one of the ties around her wrist, the one secured around the hand that has the scar on it from when we made our blood promise; the promise we made to be together forever. "Cause me pain? Agony? Hurt me until I take my last breath and die?" I unhitch one of the knots and loosen the fabric, moving slowly, carefully. She watches my face instead of my hands, trying to act tough; but still, she looks so lost, just like when I first met her. "Do you think you could do it?"

She nods her head while her eyes remain fastened on mine, yet there's hesitancy in them. "I can do anything I want to, and the thing is, you can't stop me."

I don't know why I do it, other then the need to devour her as I make her mine again. Force the possession out of her and bring her back. Do something other than feel so helpless. I hate feeling helpless. So, in a desperate panic, I lean down and kiss her passionately, half expecting her to bite me. She doesn't, though.

She just lies there beneath me, her hand twitching restlessly in the bind I have untied. Her chest is crashing against mine as she inhales and exhales ravenously, her body heat intoxicating as she rolls her hips, rubbing ever so slightly against mine. It's mind blowing, the way she makes me feel; the heat flowing between us, the sparks, near explosion. I'm one step away from ripping her clothes off and fucking her. I'm nearly being driven mad by the feel of her, almost completely forgetting the situation as her intoxicating taste overpowers me. Then I feel her shift and her hand slips out of the bind.

I have seconds to respond as her hand finds my neck and wraps around it. She pulls me toward her, looking me in the eye as she digs her fingers inward. "You think I'm weak?" she questions in a low voice that doesn't even sound like it belongs to her. "That a fucking kiss is going to stop me from doing what's burning in my blood? Stop the painful desire to spill your blood out? Stop the throbbing need to end your life?"

When she tugs me even closer, our foreheads slamming together, I don't bother fighting it as my body falls on top of hers. My weight lands on her as she leans up and nips my lip, sucking it into her mouth and grazing her teeth across it. Blood pools out and the taste of salt and rust floods my mouth. "You like me better this way, any-way; if you'd just admit it to yourself," she whispers against my lips.

My veins are pulsating under her rough touch as I gasp for air quietly, not wanting to give her the satisfaction of seeing me weak and powerless. "You have no idea what I like," I choke, gripping handfuls of the blanket beside her head, trying to hold my weight up off of her in a lame attempt to get away.

She tries to wiggle her hand out of the other bind as she continues to strangle me, her eyes filled with both desire and terror. She wants to do this, yet she doesn't want to, which means my Gemma still lies inside there some-where, and I have to get her out somehow. The only way I can think of is to push her to her limits. Let her get close to killing me. Let her think I'm about to die. Then maybe her true feelings will come out and override what my father has done to her.

I've seen this done once when a Keeper became pos-sessed by a Lost Soul, which is basically a mummy that possesses and steals souls. A Witch brought the Keeper back by testing them; pushing them to the point where they were either going to have to completely give into the Lost Soul's possession or fight their way back. I know Gemma is a fighter, but the problem is that I don't know her true feelings for me, or if she even has any at all. I guess I'm about to find out.

I let her keep choking me; suffocating me, strangling me. I see life in her eyes flicker then diminish. Her emotions turn on and off. She's conflicted. This is good. It means she cares about me; has feelings for me; wants me enough that she's not sure she really desires my death. The idea both enthralls me and scares the shit out of me. All my life, I've felt nothing for anyone, and that's how I've liked it because feelings equal hurt. Pain. Loneliness. Shut everyone out and no one can hurt you. Turn it off and you'll be stronger. That's what I've been taught.

That was the great thing about dating Stasha. I never had any feelings for her. She didn't make me happy. Piss me off. Get under my skin. Floor me to the point where I felt like I was going to explode.

Gemma on the other hand… She does all of that and more. My emotions are so tangled up inside because I want her so fucking much, yet I'm afraid to want her so badly.

"You can't do it," I choke as my breath dwindles, my lungs constricting. It's becoming harder to breathe. The room is spinning and the lights above our heads are dimming. "You care for me too much."

"Stop saying that," she growls, her face reddening with anger.

"No," I say, however it sounds more like a groan. "I won't."

"Shut up!"

"You care for me. Admit it."

She leans even closer and speaks slowly. "Think whatever you want, but the truth is, I feel nothing for you." Her grip tightens. Suddenly the lights in her eyes turn off and there's nothing there anymore. No life inside. No emotion. No Gemma. Maybe I've jumped to conclusions. Perhaps I've been wrong. Maybe she doesn't care about me like I've thought she does. And if so, I'm not sure what to do about it now that I've realized how much I care about her. There's no reversing that. She owns me now.

It feels like I should fight back, but I don't. I have no idea whether it's because I'm confused or if I'm simply so dizzy that my strength is gone. I start to fall. Sink into darkness. I think I'm dying and Gemma is the one doing it—killing me. I can't breathe and the buzzing of the sparks is fizzling. I need to fight, yet I feel nothing...

"I think I might love you," Gemma whispers in my ear as she holds onto me. "But I'm confused."

"About what?" I ask, trying not to smile as I kiss her neck, my eyes shut, the cool air brushing across my skin as I breathe in her scent; lavender and vanilla. "About love?"

"Yes," she says softly. "I'm not sure if what I'm feeling is that. Love or something else... can you tell me?"

I tense, my eyes remaining shut. "Tell you what?"

"What love is?" she whispers with a desperate plea in her voice, begging me to explain it to her, begging me to understand it.

I open my mouth to say something, but no noise comes out. I want to tell her everything — exactly what I feel — but I hesitate. Confused. Terrified. If I say it aloud, then everything changes. I'll no longer be what I am. I'll be weak. Vulnerable. She'll have the power to break me, just like everyone else in my life has. My father. My mother.

"Gemma, I..." I trail off, pulling back to look at her, but I can't see anything except darkness. It's everywhere, yet I know she's still there because I can feel the faint heat of the sparks and the touch of her breath.

"You don't love me, do you?" she sounds on the verge of tears. "Oh, my God, I'm so stupid."

No, you're not, I want to say, but my lips are fastened, my voice dead. I want to shout that I do love her, however for some reason I can't go to that place where I surrender.

And with each second that slips by, I feel her drifting away...

Chapter 5

(Alex)

I've only blacked out once that I can remember.

My father thought that the best way to teach me how to swim was to row me out into the middle of the lake and make me get into the water. After that, he left me there, saying the fear would force my swimming instincts to kick in because up until that point I had seemed to lack them. I was around ten years old, and although I had a good grasp on my emotions by then, I was still scared shitless as I struggled to stay afloat in the cold water while my father rowed away toward the shore. I gave a good fight, though; fought until the very end. I kept my eyes on the castle in the distance, hoping that if I stared at it, that somehow it'd come closer to me or I to it. Eventually it began to disappear; to slip out of my sight. I couldn't hold myself up above the water anymore, so I started to sink. Water filled my lungs. My heart struggled to keep beating. I ended up blacking out. I thought I would die— thought that I'd never see the sky, the land, the castle again—and the scariest part of that was that there was very little fear in that thought.

I did wake up again, though; on the shore, coughing up water with the sky above me. I thought it was my father who'd saved me, that he'd seen that I wasn't going to be able to swim and had come back to rescue me; that he cared enough about me that he didn't want me to die. But it wasn't. Aislin had been the one who swam out and saved me.

My father had been enraged. At me for giving up. At Aislin for helping me. He'd said we were useless. That we'd never amount to anything. That he wished I'd died instead of giving up. I should have been angry at him, but instead, I felt ashamed. I spent the next week in the lake, sinking and nearly drowning until, finally, I was able to swim.

I've tried not to rely on anyone ever since; tried to never be weakened by human emotion.

***

"Can you hear me?" someone says through the haziness in my head. "Nod your head if you can?"

I try to wobble my head around, but I can't find the strength to do it, so instead, I lie wherever I am, my body as heavy as cement.

"Jesus, Alex," they say and I recognize the voice—Aislin. "I thought you were stronger than this?"

I want to retort with an insult, but my lips feel weighted, sealed together. I attempt to lift my hand, yet again, I have no motion in my body.

"Oh, for the love of God." She sounds more irritated than worried, which is typical. Aislin and I have always had one of those brother-sister relationships where we argue a shitload and get annoyed easily with one another.

Seconds later, I feel water splash across my face, which is ice cold of course. I'm jolted awake, my eyes shooting open. I instantly recognize where I am—on the floor of the bedroom where I've tied Gemma up. Aislin is standing above me with an empty cup in her hand. Her eyebrows are raised and her hair is singed at the ends, which means she's recently done a spell that's backfired, so nothing new.

"Thanks," I say sarcastically as I sit up, wiping the water from my face with the back of my hand.

"You're welcome," she replies in an upbeat tone as she sets the cup down on top of the dresser.

I get to my feet, vertigo still evident, and the room sways, throwing me off balance. I stick out my hand and brace myself against the bedpost. "Where the hell have you been?" I ask, glancing at the bed where Gemma is laying with her eyes closed. I'd worry she's dead, but I can see her chest rising and falling with her breath. She looks at peace, sleeping, but the question is, why? What happened after I passed out that has made her go under?

And why did I dream what I did… it didn't even feel like a dream. It felt more real than this moment right now.

Aislin touches her hair as she frowns. "I ran into a bit of a problem at the Wicca Shop."

I blink my eyes a few times then let go of the bedpost when I get my bearings. "Why am I not surprised? Trouble seems to center around you."

She aims me a disgruntled look and then looks at Gemma. "Like you're doing any better. What the hell happened after I left?"

I sit down on the foot of the bed beside Gemma's feet, feeling the electricity, which is surprisingly quiet; it's barely there, fading. It makes me nervous. "She's possessed." I lean over and point to the mark on her arm. "And from what I picked up, our lovely father put this on her," I tell her, my voice dripping with bitterness.

She shakes her head, her eyes enlarged. "But how is that even possible?"

I shrug and then explain to her in detail what little I know, hoping she'll have a magical solution to fix this. I can tell though, by the time that I'm finished explaining stuff to her that she's as lost as I am on what we should do,.

"I can't believe she attacked you." She sinks down on a chair in the corner near the door that leads to the back.

"Why?" I ask, leaning in so that my hip is against Gemma's leg, if for no other reason than because I desperately need to touch her. I get a nip of sparks, but softer than usual. "She's possessed by evil. It'd be weird if she didn't attack me."

"I know, but..." she mulls over something deeply. "It's just crazy. I mean the mark... it's only supposed to show up on those that are evil."

"She said she had evil blood in her," I explain. "But I'm guessing that's the words of our father, not her."

She pulls a hesitant face. "How can you be sure, though? I mean, we hardly know anything about her family... her mother was so secretive about her father. For all we know, he could be Malefiscus."

"Watch it," I warn. "Don't you dare go there."

She slumps back in the chair and puts her arms on the armrests. "I have to because you're sure as hell not going to. You never think clearly when it comes to her."

I want to yell at her and deny what she's saying, but the truth is, I don't have a clear head when it comes to Gemma. Between my lust, befuddled emotions, and the sparks all connected to her, my head's foggy every time she's near me. It fucking sucks, yet at the same time, I like the feeling of no control…. I'm extremely conflicted.

"So do you think you can figure out a spell to take the mark off her arm?" I ask, changing the subject as Gemma lets out a loud exhale, trying to roll on her side in her sleep. The binds around her legs and one of her arms restrain her from moving too much, though, and she ends up on her back again.

"Well, I might have," Aislin says, impatiently tapping her foot on the floor, "if your ex-girlfriend hadn't stolen my spell book. I mean, what the hell was that about? She's not even a witch." She mutters something under her breath, shaking her head in annoyance. "You know, I've always hated Stasha."

"You and everyone else," I tell her. "Including me."

"Then why did you date her?"

"Why does anyone date anyone? Because they're bored."

"That logic is a little misconstrued, Alex," she says with a sigh. "Jesus, you're so messed up sometimes." She rubs her hand across her face as she thinks for what feels like hours when in reality it's probably just a few minutes. She glances at Gemma then gets up from the chair, walks over to the bed, and examines her. "I'm surprised you used your little gift on her."

"I didn't want to," I say, getting to my feet and wandering to the other side of the bed to stroke Gemma's cheek with my finger. "But it was my only choice."

"Yeah, but it's her… despite how you act, when it comes to Gemma, you've always been… How do I put this? …kinder than you are to most people."

My initial instinct is to argue, but deep down I know she's right. "There's nothing wrong with being nice sometimes," I say defensively. I then trace a line down the palm of my hand, remembering when we made the promise in a desperate act to hold onto our friendship at time where I could feel it slipping away all because of my father. "Besides, sometimes it feels like I have to be that way with her."

Aislin glances up at me with a questioning look in her eyes. "Because of the promise?"

"Maybe." I don't say anything further because I don't want to explain it to her; that I don't think what I'm feeling has anything to do with magic. That it's my emotions making me feel obligated. Hell, obligation may not even be the best word either since I *want* to protect Gemma no matter what.

"Well, I think it's good that you're finally showing signs of being human," she says with a small smile.

"If you say so," I mutter, letting my hand fall to my side.

Aislin sighs then tips her head to the side, returning her attention to Gemma, who starts to stir, wiggling her fingers as if to get out. Instead, she lets out a quiet breath and relaxes as she drapes her one untied hand over her forehead, revealing the scar on the palm of her hand. Aislin leans over to study it, then her eyes land on me and light up. "I think I have an idea."

"Good because I think I'm tapped out of them." I sit down on the bed, rake my fingers through my hair, and rest my head in my hands. "Which is a first for me, and I'm not a fan."

"Oh, quit being a baby. You don't always have to be the one to save the day," she says, rounding the bed and stopping in front of where I'm sitting. "What I'm thinking of isn't going to take off the mark, but maybe it will get rid of the power in it temporarily until I can find a more permanent spell."

"Okay." I raise my head and glance over my shoulder at Gemma lying on the bed. God, it's so fucked up, but she looks so sexy now; eyes shut, soft breaths escaping her parted lips. I want her—I've always wanted her. "Get it done then."

Aislin bites on her fingernails. "It's not something I have to do." She reluctantly aims a finger at me. "It's something you have to do. Or at least it'll work better if you do it, I think."

My brows furrow as I stand up from the bed. "What do you mean?"

"I mean," she opens her hand, palm up, and traces a line across her palm, "That you're going to make a blood promise with her."

I roll my eyes and shake my head with disappointment because, there for a moment, I've thought she had a real plan. "That's not going to work. Blood Promises aren't more powerful than the Mark of Malefiscus."

Now she rolls her eyes. "Maybe under normal circumstances, but with you two, I'm betting it'll work. The connection between you is way more intense than any normal connection out there. You've both got the star in you and you have a lot of power." She taps her finger against her lip. "I'm guessing with the right promise, we can release her for a bit from the power of the mark."

"What promise it going to do that?" I gape at her, not buying into her theory that this is going to work.

"One you're not going to like," she says, twisting a strand of her hair around her finger as she stares at Gemma. "Then again, maybe you will."

"Which is?"

"Getting her to promise to listen to someone else."

My jaw drops. "You want me to seal her to a blood promise where she has listen to me—where she's be under my control? That's fucked up."

"It's better than the alternative," she says with a shrug. "And it's all I've got at the moment."

"I'm not so sure about that. Making her… controlling her like that… it's wrong… She's already had too much of it in her life."

Her brow arches with speculation. "You really do care for her, don't you?"

Squirming uncomfortably from her accusation, I change the subject. "Even if I did make the promise, how are we supposed to get her to recite whatever I say? There's no way. Not when she's under the control of the mark."

She ponders over this for a while, as if the thought hasn't even crossed her mind until then. The longer it goes on, the more puzzled she appears. My hope in finding an easy way out of this is dwindling. Nothing's ever easy, though. I should know that by now.

"I have a better idea," I tell her, loosely using the word *better*. Because my idea isn't better at all, but it's doable.

"And what's that?" she asks, confused.

I shrug, like what I'm about to say isn't a big deal. "An emotional exorcism."

She's already shaking her head. "No way in hell. It's too risky."

"Well, it's a good thing I like risks." I try to force a cocky smile, but I miss the mark. I can act tough all I want, but what I'm proposing that we do to handle the situation is sort of terrifying.

"It's not even the risk, though," she says. "The last time someone did it, they died."

"Well, death's a risk I'm willing to take to save her." As soon as I say it, I know it's the truth, and the truth is more terrifying than I ever could have imagined.

I care enough for Gemma that I'm willing to risk my own life to free hers.

Chapter 6

(Alex)

"No. There's no way we're going to do that." Aislin paces the length of the room, shaking her head as she stares at the floor. She's been doing it since I divulged my plan of almost killing myself while Gemma's awake in the hopes that it'll bring her back.

"It can't hurt to try," I say, watching her from the bed, more stressed than I have ever been.

She stops in the middle of the room and puts her hands on her hips. "Can't hurt to try? You could freaking die, Alex. And besides," she starts pacing again, folding her arms, "she already tried to kill you and it didn't bring her back."

"It did something," I argue, drawing a line up and down Gemma's leg, missing her so much that it's driving me crazy. It's amazing how even when we're close, I want to be closer. All those years apart and I never stopped thinking about her. Then we ran into each other at her grandparent's house, and even though I thought it was forbidden, I also knew right then and then that I had to have her in my life again. "She's been unconscious ever since."

"Yeah, but—" she begins to protest again, but I interrupt her.

"Aislin, this isn't up for debate," I tell her, getting to my feet and cutting her off her pacing in the center of the room. "I'm doing this with or without your help."

She huffs in aggravation, yet I already know she'll help me. Aislin's just that way; when it all comes down to it, she gives in.

"Fine." She surrenders, throwing her hands in the air exasperatedly. "We'll try it, but I really hope you know what you're doing."

the her heart. "One shot of it right here and your dead."

Dead. As soon as she says it, reality crashes over me. I'm really going to do this, and if it all comes down to it—if it takes me actually jabbing a needle full of death into my heart to bring her back—I'll do it. I'll do whatever it takes, and it's startling how okay I am with it; sacrificing my life to save hers.

"I might be able to bring you back if you use it," Aislin says quietly, lowering her hand to her side. "As long as I don't wait too long, but I can't promise anything."

"Let's just hope I don't have to use it," I say. "That she'll come back to me before it gets that far."

She looks as doubtful as I feel but nods anyway and then leaves the room. And all I can do is wait with thoughts of death haunting my mind.

***

I wait with Gemma while Aislin goes to make her potion. My head is in a really fucked-up, weird place right now, swarming with emotions that I barely understand. She means so much to me—I don't get it. How can I go

65

from not caring about anything to caring about one person so much?

I'm stroking Gemma's hair, lost in my thoughts, when her eyelids lift open. The sunlight from outside hits them, and for the briefest moment she looks like my Gemma, but as quickly as the look appears, it fades.

"What the hell?" She jerks back from my hand, swinging her free arm at me. "What are you doing?" She starts bucking her body up and down and I seriously about loose it,

Now is not the time to get a fucking hard on, I think to myself as I lean over and grab her arm, attempting to restrain her. She tries to bite me as I wrap the tie around her wrist and tie it securely.

"Alex, what are you doing?" she says, panic in her voice. I pause because she almost looks and sounds like her old self. "Please untie me. This hurts."

I search her eyes, trying to look for signs that maybe she's come back to me. Perhaps when she choked me it brought her back. "I don't care if it hurts," I say cautiously, my hand still on her arm.

She pouts out her lip which Gemma has unintentionally done on a couple of occasions, and I about lose it. She's too innocent for her own good. "But it hurts," she whines.

"It's supposed to hurt," I reply, leaning over her quivering body to touch the mark on her arm. The ink looks as defined as it did before, so she has to still be possessed, doesn't she?

"You want to hurt me?" She frowns. "But you've already hurt me so much in the past."

"I don't want to hurt you." I touch the triangular mark with my fingertip. "But I do want to hurt who's controlling you at the moment."

Her forehead creases with confusion. "Who's controlling me?"

I can't read her at all. She looks genuinely baffled, but at the same time the mark is still there. "My father." I trace the mark. "The one who put this on you."

She shakes her head, her eyes glossed over in perplexity. "I don't understand… Alex, I'm so confused…" She angles her chin up and looks at her tied wrist. "Why do you have me tied up?"

Her gaze lands back on me, her lavender eyes looking so full of life, lacking possession. It makes me want to untie her then claim her as my own, which is messed up on so many different levels.

"Alex, please untie me." She lifts her head up and leans into me, pressing her chest against mine. Her lips are just inches away from me and the compulsion of the sparks causes me to do something stupid. I lean closer to her—just within reach—wanting her so badly that I can't take it.

Need. Want. Need.

"Untie me," she entices, her warm breath touching my lips, smothering me, making any rational thoughts go hazy. "And I'll let you do whatever you want to me," she whispers before sealing her lips to mine. Sparks zap at my lips, hot and fiery, as her tongue slips deeply into my mouth, devouring me even as it begs me to take over and have my way with her. It's like she can read my mind, see my thoughts, and feel how much I want to take control of her.

A thousand thoughts flood my mind; leaving the ropes on her, ripping her clothes off, thrusting inside her over and over again until she screams out my name and bites at my flesh. I want it more than anything, but the sheer fact that she's saying she'll give it to me, lets me know this isn't Gemma. Gemma is always nervous. Cautious. Innocent. She doesn't trust me enough to own her like that.

So as much as it kills me, I pull back and break the kiss. As soon as my mouth leaves hers, she lets out a growl. "Did you really think I wouldn't know?" I stand up from the bed and walk around to the foot of the bed, gripping the bars. "That it's not her in there?"

"What do you mean?" she asks, still trying to play innocent, wiggling her arms and legs. "Alex, please let me go! You're starting to scare me!" she cries, thrusting her legs with so much force the ties start to unravel.

My eyes stay on her as I get up on the bed and crawl over her, sitting on her legs to immobilize them. "I know you're still possessed, so quit with the innocent act."

"Alex, I don't know what you're talking about." Hot tears spill down her cheeks. "Please, these ropes are hurting me."

I shake my head, even though the sight of tears in her eyes makes my heart ache. "That's not going to work on me, so you can keep crying, but it's just a waste of time."

She instantly stops crying, the emotion draining from her face. "Well, aren't you clever?"

"And there you are." I lean over her body, sweeping my fingers across her tear stained cheek. "Don't worry, I'm going to get that mark off of you."

She starts to laugh. "You can't win this one, Alex Avery. This mark has more power than you can even comprehend."

I want to ask her a thousand questions about the mark's power and what she knows about it. Right now she probably has an insight into my father's thoughts in a way and probably knows more than I do. The problem is, because of the mark, I'm certain she can't say anything.

The longer I remain silent, the bigger her smirk grows on her face as she stares up at me. "Not so cocky now," she says with irresistible arrogance in her demeanor.

I'm about to climb off of her... or kiss her... I'm not sure which, when the door creaks open. Aislin enters with a syringe in her hand, her cheeks flushed, and her hair burnt and two or three inches shorter than when she left about a half an hour ago.

"Jesus, that's a hard spell to pull off," she says, fanning her hand in front of her face as I climb off Gemma and get up.

"Why's she here?" Gemma growls, exposing her teeth like she's a savage vampire as she glares at Aislin. "And what the hell does she have in her hand.

"Ever heard of an emotional exorcism?" Aislin raises the syringe with a proud smile on her face.

Gemma snickers. "I'm not a demon or a spirit. You're going to have to do better than that." She lifts her hips and starts nipping her teeth in my direction.

Aislin's eyes widen as she looks at me in horror. "Wow. She's really mean."

"She's not Gemma," I remind her, and then stick out my hand, noting my palms are a little bit damp with sweat. I'm nervous, another emotion I'm not accustom to.

Aislin is reluctant to hand over the syringe, eyeballing it with hesitancy as she holds it in her hand. "Are you absolutely sure about this?" she asks.

"I have to do it," I say because it's all I *can* say. No, I don't want to do it, but sometimes that's how life works.

Tears fall from Aislin's eyes as she hands the syringe over. "I might not be able to bring you back... If you completely go through with it and if I can't... then you'll be... you'll be..."

"Dead," I finish for her, my fingers wrapping around the syringe. "I understand the consequences, let's just hope it doesn't go that far."

Still crying, Aislin backs into the corner, hugging her arms around herself as tears stream down her cheeks. Aislin has always been a little overly dramatic in my opinion; too weepy and emotionally attached to people. I've never really understood it until now; why some people can affect you more than others.

"Are you insane?" Gemma laughs maliciously as she takes in the sight of the syringe in my hand when I turn around and face her. "You think that will kill me?"

I shake my head, grasping the syringe tightly in my hand. "No. I know it won't kill you because I'm not going to use it on you." With a deep breath, I bite off the cap on the needle and spit it onto the floor. Then I aim the needle at his chest. "It's going to kill me."

Something sparks inside her eyes, like fire, blazing intensely. "You won't do it. Humans fear death more than anything."

I inch the needle closer to my chest until the tip is poking the fabric of my shirt. "Not this human, and I think the real Gemma knows me enough to know that's the truth."

"The real Gemma is dead," she snarls. "So this is just a wasted effort.

"Well, if that's true, then I guess I'm about to find out," I say, hating that my voice is a little unsteady.

"I'm calling your bluff." She arches her eyebrows challengingly, but I can see the anxiousness hidden beneath her confidence. "You don't have it in you to go through with it."

"You think so, huh?" My hand trembles as I summon another breath, then giving myself no time to back out, I sink the needle into his skin. Blood pools out and my heart hammers in my chest. Just one push of the end and death

74

will be injected into my body. I'm more terrified than I thought I would be, but mainly because I fear I'll never see Gemma again; that she'll be left unprotected in the world and something will happen to her.

"Say you care for me," I demand, getting close to her, wanting to evoke emotion out of her. "Tell me not to do it."

She shakes her head swiftly. "Never."

I put my thumb on the end of the syringe, ready to push. "Then I guess this is good-bye." Shit. I can't believe I'm about to go through with this, and all I can do is hope that Aislin can bring me back.

"Then do it," she says as she presses her lips together and waits.

Sparks are going crazy between us, full force, either feeding off my emotions or hers. I'm hoping hers, for the sake of making this sacrifice worth it.

"Get ready, Aislin," I say with my eyes locked on Gemma. Then, summoning a shaky breath, I push the end of the syringe with my thumb.

Aislin lets out a hysterical weep. "Alex! Stop!"

But it's too late. The medicine is injected into my body and courses through my veins; potent, liquid fire that burns and boils my blood. I can't think. Hear. See anything. My breath is leaving me. I can no longer feel my heart beating. I'm about to die. Images flood my head, one's I'm familiar with, ones I've never seen before.

Gemma and I. Our hideout. Violet flowers she used to pick for me all the time. Dancing in a field with her. Kissing her, touching her. Love. Blood Promise. Blood-bonded eternally. Forever.

Someone screams at the top of their lungs. "*Stop!* Stop! Stop! Stop. It's me. It's Gemma. Alex, stop!"

"Gemma…" I wrench the needle out of my heart, blood drizzling through my shirt. I'm panting, skin pale, dying. I heard her voice—I heard Gemma—which means it worked. It had to have worked. And now I'm dying, leaving her. "Damn it…" My breath slips away, and as my heart takes its last beat, I collapse to the floor.

Epilogue

(Gemma)

It happens so quickly that I don't have time to process it. One minute my brain is full of haziness where I can only see one single thought—kill Alex—and then suddenly I'm free, my heart flooding with emotions.

Pain. Longing. Need. Sadness. I see so many things. Alex and I. Our hide out. Violet flowers. Dancing in a field. Blood Promise. Forever.

Everything I've ever felt in my past, before my emotions were erased, surges through back to me and jumpstarts my emotions.

I scream at the top of my lungs. *"Stop!* Stop! Stop! Stop. It's me. It's me. Alex, stop!"

But it's too late. He gags as he pulls the needle out of his heart. Gasping for air, his skin pallid, eyes wide. Seconds later, he crumples to the floor.

A blood-curdling scream rips from my lips. "Aislin! Untie me! *Please.* He can't die now!" *I did this. This is all my fault. No. Help. Stop. Please. God, it hurts so much.*

Aislin buckles over Alex's body with her head tucked down as she utters a chant under her breath, over and over again. Her hand glows red as she presses it to his heart. I realize she's doing a spell, hopefully one that will bring him back. However, the longer it goes on, the more my hope crumbles. After a while, Aislin gets quiet, tears still falling from her eyes as she glances up at me.

"He's dead, Gemma. He's dead," she whispers softly as the glow from her hand fades.

"No, he's not!" I cry as I tug on the ties around my arms and legs. "Aislin, please untie me. I need to be with him."

She finally is able to get up, and then she moves over to me, her eyes swollen; tears streaming down her cheeks. She unfastens the ties around my wrists, her fingers shaking. As soon as she gets the last one, I spring upright and scramble over to where Alex is lying on the floor. His eyes are open, though distant and blank; his arms and legs are sprawled on the floor. He's not breathing. I check his pulse with my fingertips. Nothing. I try to feel the sparks. Nothing. I feel nothing.

I vaguely hear Aislin say something to me, but I can't make out her words. There's so much pain. Emptiness. I feel like I'm being pushed down from it. Sinking. Falling. Dying.

***

There's a frozen lake before me and icicles dangle from the leafless tree branches. The dark sky casts a shadow over the icy land and the air is as chilly as death. Alex's arms are wrapped tightly around me as we stand near the edge of the frozen water, holding onto one another as if our lives depend on it.

"We'll be all right, won't we?" I ask him, but he doesn't respond.

A gentle breeze blows through my hair and the silence around us makes the world feel desolate, hollow, and empty. At the moment, though, I feel at whole; at peace, calm.

I tip my head back and look up at him to tell him my worries, but he shushes me as he brushes my hair away from my face. "It will be all right," he whispers, but his voice is unsteady.

My lips part to argue, but a crackle rises through the air and sucks the words from my lips. Moments later, tall, cloaked figures emerge from the trees surrounding us.

"Death Walkers." I look at Alex in terror. "What do we do?"

He sweeps my hair back again and pulls me closer to him. "It will be all right," he whispers again. "Just trust me."

I feel warmth and pain. Heat and agony. Then suddenly I'm suffocated by light. Yet for some reason, it feels like everything will be okay.

Gripping onto him, I take a deep breath and let the warmth engulf me, allowing myself to get taken away from the world as I hold onto Alex, refusing to let go. There's a soft tug and I can feel him slipping away, though. I let out a scream, but I get lost in the light.

***

"*Gemma*," a voice calls out to me. "*Can you hear me?*"

My body tenses as light encircles me. "Who's there?"

"Come toward me," the voice echoes around me.

I lift my hand to my forehead and try to shield my eyes from the blinding light, but I still can't see a thing. "Whoever you are, I can't see you. The light's too bright."

"Yes, you can," the voice assures me. "You just have to look harder."

The voice sounds familiar, but I'm certain that it doesn't belonged to Nicholas, even though it seems like something he would say to fuck with my head. The voice is much deeper, though, and sounds older and wiser.

I blink a few times and the light begins to dim. Slowly at first, and then more quickly, until there's nothing left other than a soft glow orbing around me. I can see my hands and arms… my feet… I start to get my bearings when, suddenly, my legs are ripped out from under me.

I fall for what seems like forever until, finally, I land on my back. My vision comes into focus and I'm shocked to my very core at what I see. A midnight-blue marble floor rests below me, a cathedral ceiling painted with intricate art above me, and tile walls made of sapphire blue and shimmering silver surround me. It's beautiful. Too beautiful.

"I have to be dead," I mutter, getting to my feet. I examine myself. My skin is pale, but that's normal, yet I can feel the air coming in and out of my lungs, my heart still beating in my chest. I have to be alive, but where the hell am I?

"Hello!" I call out, turning in a circle as I take in a row of columns on each side of me forming a hallway that leads to a colossal statue.

I walk toward the statue, taking each step carefully, afraid that any second someone—or something—will jump out from behind one of the columns. Quite honestly, though—deep down—I think I'm hoping Alex will appear from somewhere. Surprise me. Tell me he's okay... that he didn't... die.

I start crying again as I reach the end, thinking about where Alex could be and if he's alive. My heart feels like it's shattered. Broken. I'm broken. Just like the statue with a crack down the center, although it's still in tact. Made of flawless, white marble and perfect edges, it forms a figure that looks like a tall man. Looking closer, there is something about the angles of the face that look familiar, and there's a crystal ball chiseled in his hand.

"What in the hell?" I lean closer, squinting at the plaque mounted on the statue's feet. As soon as I read it, my pulse quickens to the point that it knocks the breath out of me. "Julian Lucas. Lucas? No. There is no way." I cover my mouth with my hand and back away. Where am I? What is this place?

"Don't worry, it's just a statue," someone says from right behind me.

I spin around and jump back when I come face-to-face with a man that has a striking resemblance to the statue, only he's alive and breathing with shoulder length, brown hair and violet eyes.

"Oh, my God, you're... you're..."

"Hello, Gemma," he says calmly. "I'm so glad you finally found me."

"But you're... how... why..." I can't form sentences. I'm in too much shock to process reality.

Thankfully, my dad understands. "Don't worry. I'm here to help you."

"Help me with what?" I finally get a full sentence out.

He smiles. "Fix the past and create a better future."

I glance around at the strange place. "What do you mean? Where am I?"

"You're in the only place I can be," he says, turning around and putting a hand on the small of my back to guide me with him as he walks forward.

I walk nervously with him, my heart still erratic in my chest. "What do you mean by fix the past?"

"I mean, we're going to do what probably seems like the impossible," he says as we walk up the tiled path. "We're going to reset time and erase some of the past to hopefully create a better future for the world."

My heart quiets inside my chest. Calms. For the briefest moment, I swear I can feel the sparks. If what he's saying is true—if we're going to erase some of the past to hopefully help the world—then maybe I can also help Alex.

Maybe I can reset it so he doesn't die.

Maybe I can bring him back.

The New York Times and USA Today bestselling author, Jessica Sorensen, lives in the snowy mountains of Wyoming. When she's not writing, she spends her time reading and hanging out with her family.

Other books by Jessica Sorensen:

The Secret of Ella and Micha (The Secret, #1)

The Fallen Star (Fallen Star Series, Book 1)

The Underworld (Fallen Star Series, Book 2)

The Vision (Fallen Star Series, Book 3)

The Promise (Fallen Star Series, Book 4)

Connect with me online: http://jessicasorensen.com

http://jessicasorensensblog.blogspot.com/

http://www.facebook.com/#!/JessicaSorensensAdultConte mporaryNovels?notif_t=page_new_likes

http://www.facebook.com/pages/Jessica-Sorensen/165335743524509

https://twitter.com/#!/jessFallenStar

Jessica Sornsen

Unbroken

Printed in Great Britain
by Amazon